Brooke
the Photographer
Fairy

by Daisy Meadows

ORCHARD

www.rainbowmagic.co.uk

The Fairyland Palace

Tippington Fountains SHOPPING CENTRE

Fashion Show

Top hats & tiaras

FASHION

HARTLEY'S

'Ice Blue' Hair Salon

TIPPINGTON TOYS

'Ice Blue' stall

Jack Frost's Spell

I'm the king of designer fashion,
Looking stylish is my passion.
Ice Blue's the name of my fashion range,
Some people think my clothes are strange.

Do I care, though? Not a bit!
My designer label will be a hit.
The Fashion Fairies' magic will make that come true:
Soon everyone will wear Ice Blue!

Contents

Photo Fiasco

"This place is so beautiful," said Kirsty Tate, gazing around at the lush green grass, the bright flowers and the potted palms. "Isn't it a funny feeling to have a garden up so high!"

She was standing in the roof garden on top of the brand-new *Tippington Fountains Shopping Centre*. The glass-fronted Roof Garden Cafe was at the

far end. Next to the cafe was a glass lift, which took visitors down to the shopping centre.

"It must be even lovelier when the sun's shining," replied her best friend Rachel Walker. "All the glass must really sparkle."

They both looked up at the grey rain clouds that were gathering overhead.

"Yes, it's such a pity that it isn't a sunny day," Kirsty agreed.

All week long, the girls had been involved in the Design-and-Make Competition at the new shopping centre.

There was a fashion show the following day to mark the end of the centre's first week.

"I think it's the best place to have a photoshoot, even if the weather isn't perfect," said Rachel with a smile.

Kirsty and Rachel's outfits had been among those selected to feature in the fashion show. Today, the winners were taking part in a photoshoot for *The Fountains Fashion News* magazine on the roof garden. Supermodel Jessica Jarvis and dress designer Ella McCauley were there too. They had been special guests at the shopping centre all week, and now they were helping the children to make sure that their colourful, imaginative clothes looked as good as possible. Kirsty was wearing the dress that she had made out of scarves, and Rachel had put on her rainbow-painted jeans.

Cam Carson, the photographer, was busily organising the winners into groups.

"I'd like you all to choose themes for your photos," she said. "It should be something that connects with your designs and means something special to you."

Kirsty turned to Rachel.

"What shall we choose?" she asked. "What fits with rainbow colours?"

"Easy," said Rachel. "Our theme should be friendship. That fits with rainbows – the fairies taught us that!"

The girls held hands and smiled at each other.

"That's perfect," Kirsty replied. "We're very lucky. I'm so glad we met each other that day on the boat to Rainspell Island."

"Me too," said Rachel.

Ever since that holiday on Rainspell
Island, the girls had shared a wonderful
secret. They were friends with the fairies,
and they often travelled to Fairyland
and helped to outwit Jack Frost and
his naughty goblins. Their friendship
had grown stronger and
stronger with every
adventure they
shared.

The other winners
were getting
ready for their
photograph to be
taken. A boy called
Dean was wearing
a space-themed
T-shirt and carrying
a model spaceship.

14

A girl called Layla had designed a football kit and had a football tucked under her arm.

"You all look wonderful," said Jessica. "Now remember, the best photographs are taken when you look happy and natural. So just try to relax and smile!"

Cam Carson picked up her camera and tucked her golden-brown hair behind her ears.

"OK, I'm ready," she said. "Who's going first?"

"Rachel and Kirsty are first on the list," said Ella, ushering them forward.

The girls put their arms around each other and smiled. But just as Cam took the photograph, Kirsty's hair blew in front of her face.

"Oops," said Cam with a laugh. "Let's try again."

She pressed the button once more and then checked the picture on the screen.

"Oh dear, you were blinking," she said to Rachel. "Third time lucky!"

16

She pressed the button again, but this time her finger was in front of the lens.

"What's the matter with me today?" she muttered.

There was a low rumble of thunder, and everyone looked up. The dark rain clouds were moving nearer.

"I'll have to use the flash," said Cam, changing the settings on her camera.

Before she could take another photo, there was a bright flash from the camera.

"Now it's going off by itself!" she said in an exasperated voice. "Just a minute, everyone. My camera

17

just doesn't seem to want to work today!"

She fiddled with the controls again, but before she could press the button there was another unexpected flash. Taken by surprise, Layla dropped her football and it bounced towards the edge of the roof. Dean tried to stop it, and skidded to a halt near the edge of the roof. He lost his grip on his model spaceship, and it crashed to the floor and broke into three pieces.

"It's not our lucky day." Cam sighed as

Dean picked up the pieces of spaceship.

"This isn't ordinary bad luck," Rachel whispered to Kirsty. "This is Jack Frost's work!"

Flashes on the Roof

Kirsty nodded, thinking about the things that had happened that week. It had all started on the first day of half-term. The girls had been whisked off to Fairyland to see their friends in a fashion show. But Jack Frost and the goblins also turned up, modelling crazy, bright-blue outfits from Jack's designer label, Ice Blue.

To everyone's horror, Jack Frost had announced that everyone would soon be wearing Ice Blue clothes – designed by him! With a bolt of icy magic, he stole the magical objects belonging to the Fashion Fairies and brought them to *Tippington Fountains Shopping Centre.*

Without their magical objects, the Fashion Fairies couldn't look after fashion in the human and fairy worlds. The girls knew that they had to do something. They had already helped five of the fairies to get their magic objects back – but there were still two more to find.

Kirsty's thoughts were interrupted by a touch of drizzle on the tip of her nose.

Cam sighed as she looked up at the grey clouds.

"Everything's going wrong today," she said. "All right, everyone, let's take a break and go inside. Perhaps it's just going to be a passing shower."

She sheltered her camera equipment under a large umbrella and then followed Jessica, Ella and the children into the Roof Garden Cafe. Kirsty and Rachel hung back and exchanged a secret glance.

"This must have something to do with Jack Frost," said Rachel.

"Yes, and his naughty goblins," Kirsty agreed. "The weather forecast didn't say anything about drizzle. It was supposed to be sunny."

"Come on, let's go inside before we get wet," said Kirsty.

They turned towards the cafe, but then Rachel grasped her friend's arm in excitement. She had caught sight of something out of the corner of her eye.

"Kirsty, look," she said, pointing at Cam's equipment.

The camera was perched on top of
a tripod, and the flash seemed to be
glowing more brightly than normal. It
was hard to see the camera behind the
golden glow.

"I would have thought Cam would
turn the flash off
while she wasn't
using it," said
Kirsty.

"That's
not a flash,"
said Rachel,
looking at
the glowing
light more closely.
"It's Brooke the
Photographer Fairy!"

Brooke smiled and waved at them.

The girls glanced back at the cafe to check that no one was watching, and then hurried over to the little fairy. She looked vibrant in her skinny jeans and tunic top, and her glossy black hair bounced as she hovered in front of them. Her dark eyes glinted with fun and excitement.

"Hello, Kirsty! Hello, Rachel! Have I interrupted a photoshoot? You both look fabulous!" she said.

"Thanks," said Kirsty with a smile.
"But it was the rain that interrupted the
photoshoot, not you. Everything seems
to be going wrong for the photographer
today."

"That's why I'm here," said Brooke.
"While my magic camera is missing,
all fashion shoots will be ruined. I was
hoping that you'd help me, just like
you've helped the other Fashion Fairies."

"Of course we
will," said
Rachel
eagerly.
"We'll do
everything
we can to
find your
magic camera."

She turned to Kirsty, who was staring over at the other side of the roof garden.

"There's something going on over there," said Kirsty. "I keep seeing lots of flashes."

"Like camera flashes?" asked Brooke.

"Yes," said Kirsty. "Look, there's another one!"

Rachel and Brooke saw a bright flash.

"That's odd," said Rachel. "Cam's supposed to be the only photographer up here this morning."

"Let's go and investigate," Brooke suggested. "I have a feeling that something funny is going on over there."

"But you mustn't be seen," said Kirsty. "There are lots of people in the cafe over there. One of them might spot you!"

"Here, hide in my bag," Rachel said,

holding open her pretty rainbow-coloured shoulder bag.

Brooke fluttered into Rachel's bag, and then the girls hurried over to the far side of the roof garden.

There were even more flashes coming from that direction now, and they could hear giggles and squawks. What on earth was going on?

Jack Frost, Supermodel!

The girls crouched down behind a row of large potted palm trees, and then cautiously peered around the green leaves. In the middle of a small clearing, Jack Frost and four goblins were having their own photo shoot!

Jack Frost was wearing an Ice Blue
jumpsuit, with wide flares and a long,
rounded collar. He had completed his
outfit with a sequinned
electric-blue cape
and a matching top
hat. He was posing
with one hand on
his hip and the
other pointing up
to the gloomy sky,
and he looked very
pleased with himself.
"You!" he bellowed
at the shortest goblin.
"Fluff up my beard!"
As the little goblin rushed forward to
obey, Jack jabbed his bony finger into the
squashy stomach of a plump goblin.

"You! Fetch me
a different hat!"
he demanded. "I
want the glittery
cowboy hat and I
want it NOW!"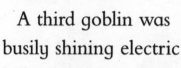
A third goblin was
busily shining electric
lights onto Jack Frost from all angles.

"Brighter!" the Ice Lord screeched.
"For a star like me, the lights should be
dazzling, you idiot!"

As the lights grew even brighter, the
drizzle stopped and a ray of sunshine fell
across Jack Frost's face. The plump goblin
handed him the cowboy hat. A skinny
goblin held up a little camera and called
out instructions to the frosty model.

"That's great!" he squawked as Jack

gave his grimacing smile. "Let's see those pearly white teeth! Give me attitude! Give me pizzazz! Who's the boss?"

"ME!" Jack Frost exclaimed, giving a massive grin and arching an eyebrow.

The photographer snapped away as

Jack Frost struck pose after pose. Brooke peeped out of Rachel's bag and gasped. Then she fluttered up to Rachel's

34

shoulder and folded
her arms across her
chest.

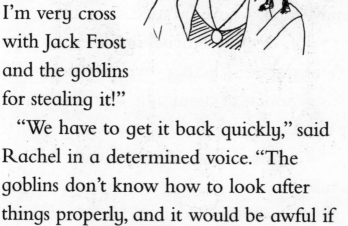

"That's my
magic camera,"
she said. "I'm
so glad we've
found it, but
I'm very cross
with Jack Frost
and the goblins
for stealing it!"

"We have to get it back quickly," said
Rachel in a determined voice. "The
goblins don't know how to look after
things properly, and it would be awful if
they broke the camera."

At that moment, the skinny goblin
nearly dropped the camera! Brooke

almost squealed out
loud, but the goblin
caught it just in time.
He put the strap
around his neck.

"That was close,"
said Kirsty. "We'd
better do something fast,
and I think I have an idea. Brooke,
can you disguise Rachel and me as
photographers? Perhaps we can move
close enough to the magic camera to get
it back."

"No problem," said Brooke with a
wink.

She waved her wand, and a fountain of
silver fairy sparkles cascaded around the
girls. A big camera appeared on a strap
around Kirsty's neck, and Rachel found

herself carrying spare lenses, a tripod and a couple of hand-held lights. Their beautiful clothes disappeared, and were replaced with bright-blue suits that looked as if they might be from Jack Frost's Ice Blue designer label.

Brooke hid in the pocket of Rachel's dazzling jacket, and then the girls took deep breaths and stepped out from behind the potted palms. They walked slowly towards the little group.

Jack Frost started shouting as soon as he saw them.

"Clear off!" he hollered. "This is a very important photoshoot and you're getting in the way. GET LOST!"

The girls ignored his rudeness and smiled at him.

"We're terribly sorry," said Kirsty. "It's just that we work for *Fashion World* magazine, and we're MASSIVE fans of your Ice Blue fashion label. We're here to take your photo for the cover of the next issue."

"But we can see you're busy, so we'll leave," Rachel added, turning away.

"WAIT!" shouted Jack Frost. "I want

to be a cover model! Come back here,
NOW!"

Kirsty and Rachel stopped, and Jack
Frost started barking orders at his goblins.

"Make my hair look more pointy!
Brush my coat! Polish my shoes!
HURRY UP, you nincompoops!"

The goblins scurried around their boss,
squawking and squealing as they tried
to follow all his instructions at once. The
smallest goblin held up a mirror and Jack
nodded, preening himself.

"Are you ready?" asked Kirsty, holding
up her camera. She just hoped that her
plan would work.

Toyshop Trouble

"This will be the most important photo of my life," said Jack. "How do I look?"

"Ooh, you look very handsome, Your Iciness," said the plump goblin.

"Then I'm ready!" said Jack Frost.

Kirsty pressed the button to take a photo, but nothing happened.

"Oh no, I think the battery must be dead," she groaned. "I don't have a spare! What am I going to do?"

"We'll just have to try again for next month's issue," said Rachel.

"I'm not WAITING!" Jack Frost shouted. "Do something!"

Rachel hid a smile. She had guessed that Jack Frost wouldn't have the patience to wait.

"Well, there is one thing we could do," said Kirsty, trying to sound as if she had just had the idea. "If your photographer would lend us his camera, we could take the photo with that."

The skinny goblin clutched the camera to his chest. Jack Frost turned to him and narrowed his cold eyes.

"Hand it over," he snapped.

"But – but – but you said…" the goblin protested.

"NOW!" roared Jack Frost.

With a jump of fright, the goblin held out the precious magic camera. Kirsty and Rachel exchanged a glance – their plan was working! Kirsty stretched out her hand, her fingers brushing the strap of the camera…

Inside Rachel's pocket, Brooke was very excited to hear that the girls were going to get the camera. She couldn't resist peeping out to see what was happening.

"STOP!" bellowed Jack Frost.

Kirsty froze and the goblin snatched back the camera. Jack Frost had seen Brooke in Rachel's jacket pocket!

Jack Frost sent a bolt of icy magic

forking towards the girls, and the camera
flew out of the goblin's hand and into
Jack's clutching fingers. Two more ice
bolts sent Kirsty and
Rachel tumbling
to the ground,
and then
he ran
past them
towards the
glass lift.
The goblins
followed as
fast as they
could, and they
all dived into the lift.
It was a tight squeeze, but they fitted in
and the doors started to close.

"Quick, stop them!" cried Rachel,

scrambling to her feet and racing after the pesky lot.

But as she reached the lift, the doors slid shut and the goblins and Jack Frost were carried downwards. The last thing Rachel saw before the lift disappeared was four goblin faces pressed up against the glass, all poking their tongues out at her.

"Oh no, we've lost them!" Kirsty

exclaimed, running up behind Rachel.

"We have to follow them!" cried
Rachel.

"We'll be quicker if you can both fly,"
said Brooke.

She glanced around to check that no
one from the cafe could see them. Then
she zoomed into the
air above the
girls and waved
her wand in
a wide circle.
Silver fairy
dust sprinkled
down on
Rachel and
Kirsty.

In a flash, the
girls were swept off

their feet and into the air. Sparkling fairy
dust coiled around them, shrinking them
until they were
the same size
as Brooke.
Gossamer
wings
fluttered on
their backs,
and they
hovered beside
Brooke and smiled
at each other.

"Ready?" Brooke asked.

"Ready!" said Kirsty and Rachel
together.

"Let's go!" Brooke cried, swooping
down the staircase.

A few seconds later, the three fairies

zipped out of
the stairwell
and into the
shopping
centre. They
flew as close
to the ceiling
as they could,
so that the crowds

of shoppers wouldn't see them. The
shopping centre was busier than ever.

"I hope we're going to be able to spot
Jack Frost and the goblins among all
these people," said Kirsty.

"Look there," said Rachel, pointing
down to the *Winter Woollies* market stall.

One of the displays had been knocked
over, and shoppers were getting tangled
up in the long woollen scarves on the

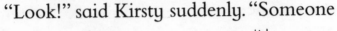

floor. Shoppers were stumbling around, bumping into each other.

"If we look for trouble, I bet Jack Frost won't be far away," Rachel continued.

"Look!" said Kirsty suddenly. "Someone

dressed in bright blue just ran into *Tippington Toys*. Let's go and see if it was Jack Frost!"

They all zoomed down to the toyshop and swooped in over a group of children. At the far end of the shop, another group of children was standing around a rocking horse. They had all put on funny hats and clothes from the dressing-up section, but something about the way they were standing made Brooke flutter closer.

"They don't look like ordinary children," said the little fairy.

As they got closer, they saw long green noses sticking out from under the hats, and bony green fingers reaching out to stroke the rocking horse's mane.

"They're goblins!" cried Rachel.

Snapping on Ice!

As the girls flew closer, they saw Jack
Frost clambering off the rocking horse.

"Take those stupid clothes off," he
snapped at the goblins. "They're not
made by my Ice Blue label, and that
means they're RUBBISH."

Grumbling, the goblins pulled off their fancy dress. Then one of them grabbed a scooter from a display nearby. The other three did the same and they all started to scoot around the shop at top speed.

Brooke, Rachel and Kirsty perched on a red kite that was hanging from the ceiling and looked down at the havoc the goblins were causing below. They rolled their scooters over the feet of other shoppers, knocked over displays and made a deafening racket.

"Look at Jack Frost!" shouted Kirsty over the hubbub.

The Ice Lord was sitting in front of a toy dressing table, playing with his hair and taking photographs of himself with Brooke's magic camera.

"He's keeping a tight hold on my camera," said Brooke with a sigh. "How are we going to get it back?"

Rachel spotted a Wendy house in the corner of the shop, and gave a little gasp.

"I think I've got an idea," she said. "Hold on to the kite and flap your wings. Flap them as hard as you can!"

Kirsty and Brooke started to flap their wings, and they felt the kite start to move beneath them, tugging on the string that suspended it from the ceiling.

"We need to make it fly towards Jack Frost," said Rachel in a breathless voice. "Flap harder!"

"I can't," groaned Kirsty.

"Perhaps my magic can help," said
Brooke.

She tapped her wand on the kite and it
started to move.

"Steer it towards Jack Frost!" Rachel
cried. "Try to chase him into the Wendy
house."

The kite gathered speed as the friends
steered it towards the toy dressing table.
Jack Frost ran off and darted into the
Wendy house, chased by Brooke and the
girls. He was trapped!

Brooke guided the kite to the floor and the three fairies hovered in the doorway.

"You're cornered," said Kirsty. "Just give back the camera and we'll let you go."

"No chance," said Jack Frost, hiding it behind his back. "This takes great photos of me, and I'm keeping it. Goblins, get over here now!"

The girls heard the sound of four

scooters being dropped on the floor,
followed by four pairs
of feet thumping
towards the
Wendy house.
The goblins
peered in
through the
window, and
then Jack
Frost flicked
his wand. There
was a loud crack
and a flash of blue magic.

"To my Ice Castle!" shouted Jack Frost.

A second later, Jack Frost and his
goblins had disappeared.

"We have to follow them, or I'll never
get my camera back," said Brooke. "Girls,

will you come to the Ice Castle with me?"

"Of course!" said Rachel.

Brooke waved her wand and said a quick spell.

"*To Jack Frost's home of snow and ice,*
Whisk us in a magic trice.
Let us follow where they flew,
But keep us safely out of view!"

There was a bright golden flash, and then the girls found

60

themselves sitting on a
frosty tree branch
in the garden
of Jack Frost's
castle.

"Look down
there," said
Kirsty, quietly.

She pointed to
a clearing among snow-
covered trees. Jack Frost and the
four goblins were standing around a large
pond, which had a waterfall pouring into
it from a high rocky crag.

"This is a much better setting for my
photoshoot," Jack Frost was saying. "All it
needs is a little extra frostiness!"

He raised his wand and ZAP! The
pond froze over. ZAP! Ice sculptures

appeared around the pond, wearing Ice
Blue designs. ZAP! The waterfall froze to
create a giant sheet of ice, like a mirror.

"What a wonderful sight," said Jack,
gazing at his reflection.

He took a few photos of himself with
the magic camera, which he didn't
seem keen to return to the goblin
photographer. Then he looked around.

"These trees aren't icy enough," he
grumbled.

ZAP! ZAP! ZAP! Tree after tree was suddenly laden down with thick, sharp icicles.

"He's turning this way!" cried Brooke. "Dodge!"

The three fairies zoomed out of the way as the tree they were sitting in was decorated with icicles. When he saw them, Jack Frost gave a yell of fury.

"What are you pesky fairies doing here?" he bellowed. "You're trying to ruin my photoshoot! I'll make you sorry you ever THOUGHT of coming here!"

Surprise Shower!

The fairies flew left and right, trying to dart out of Jack Frost's way as he zapped at them with his wand. The sculptures cracked and exploded as the ice bolts struck them. The pond melted and icicles plunged to the ground. The goblins had to dive out of the way to avoid being hit.

"Kirsty! Brooke!" Rachel shouted over the squeals and squawks of the goblins. "Meet me at the waterfall!"

The three fairies
zoomed towards
the frozen
waterfall and
swooped behind
it, hidden from
Jack Frost for a
moment.

"Do you have a plan?" panted Kirsty.

Rachel nodded and hurriedly started to
whisper to the others.

"Come out from behind my waterfall!"
Jack Frost screeched. "I'll turn you all
into ice sculptures! I'll zap you into next
week!"

Rachel peeped around the side of the
waterfall.

"He's pretty close," she whispered.
"*Now!*"

Brooke waved her wand and the frozen waterfall melted. Brooke's magic sent a shower of icy water gushing down on top of Jack Frost!

"YOWWEEEEEE!" he screamed.

In shock, he dropped the camera and Kirsty swooped down, catching it just before it hit the ground. Rachel followed her, and together they managed to lift the camera up to where Brooke was hovering. As soon as she touched it, the camera shrank back to its proper fairy size.

Dripping wet and
furious, Jack Frost
shook his fist at the
three fairies, who
were fluttering just
out of his reach.
"You haven't won!"
he raged. "I've still got
one of your precious magical
objects, and while I've got that, I can still
spoil things in the fashion world!"

"We're not going to let you do that!"
said Rachel.

Before Jack Frost could think of a
retort, Brooke waved her wand and the
three fairies were caught up in a swirl
of fairy dust. When it disappeared, they
found themselves on the shopping centre
roof garden once again.

The rain had stopped and the sun
was coming out from behind the clouds.
Kirsty and Rachel followed Brooke out
of sight behind some tall, leafy plants.

"I'd better change you back to normal,"
said Brooke. "Now that the sun has come
out, your photoshoot can go ahead.
Besides, I have to return to Fairyland and
tell the other Fashion Fairies about our
adventure!"

She waved her wand and turned
Rachel and Kirsty back
to their usual size.
Their Ice Blue suits
had disappeared,
and they were
once again
wearing their own
colourful designs.

"Goodbye," said
Brooke, fluttering
in front of them.
"And thank you
both – I'm so
happy to have my
magic camera back
at last."

"We loved helping
you," Kirsty replied.
"Goodbye, Brooke!"

Brooke waved and then
twirled upwards, faster and faster, until
she was just a golden blur. She vanished
in a flutter of wings, leaving behind
a dazzling spray of fairy dust that
shimmered like a firework display.

"Rachel! Kirsty!" called Jessica, making
the girls jump.

The girls stepped out from behind the plants and saw Jessica, Cam, Ella and the other winners standing outside the cafe. Dean had fixed his spaceship, and Layla had her football back.

"Ready to give the photoshoot another try?" asked Cam.

Everyone nodded, and Cam asked Dean and Layla to pose first. This time, the camera worked perfectly, and nothing else went wrong.

"Fantastic!" exclaimed Cam, snapping shot after shot. "Brilliant! These look great!"

When Rachel and Kirsty's turn arrived, they posed in front of the potted palms with their arms around each other's shoulders. Just as Cam was about to press the button, something wonderful happened – a rainbow appeared in the sky behind the girls!

"What a gorgeous natural backdrop for the shot!" exclaimed Cam. "These photos are going to be perfect for the special issue of *Fountains Fashion News.*"

"I can't wait for the fashion show!" said

Ella. "Looking at all of you, I can tell that it's going to be absolutely fantastic."

Kirsty, Rachel, Dean and Layla smiled at each other.

"It'll be awesome," said Dean.

"Tomorrow is going to be so much fun," added Layla.

Rachel and Kirsty hoped that she was right. However, there was still one more magical object to get back from Jack Frost. A worried frown appeared on Kirsty's face as she thought about it. Rachel grinned at her best friend and squeezed her hand.

"We won't let Jack Frost ruin the fashion show," she whispered. "Don't worry, Kirsty. The Fashion Fairies can rely on us!"

**Now it's time for Kirsty and
Rachel to help...**

Lola the Fashion Show Fairy

Read on for a sneak peek...

Kirsty Tate was *very* excited. Today, she
and her best friend Rachel Walker were
taking part in a fashion show! Not only
that, they would be wearing outfits they
had designed and made themselves, after
entering a special competition held at
Tippington Fountains Shopping Centre
earlier that week.

"I hope I don't trip over on the
catwalk," Rachel giggled as she, Kirsty
and her parents walked to their meeting
point in the shopping centre. "Knowing
me, I'll fall flat on my face and totally
embarrass myself."

74

"No, you won't," Kirsty reassured her, squeezing her hand. "You'll be brilliant. And everyone will love your rainbow jeans, I just know it."

Rachel smiled at her. "I'm so glad we're doing this together," she said.

"Me too." Kirsty grinned. "All of our best adventures happen when we're together, don't they?"

The two girls exchanged a look, their eyes sparkling. Unknown to anyone else, they shared an amazing secret. They were friends with the fairies, and had enjoyed lots of wonderful, magical fairy adventures with them. Sometimes, the girls had even been turned into fairies themselves, and been able to fly!

This week, Kirsty was staying with Rachel's family for half-term and once again, the two friends had found

themselves magically whisked away
to Fairyland when a brand-new
fairy adventure began. They'd been
invited to see a fairy fashion show but
unfortunately it had been hijacked
by naughty Jack Frost and his goblin
servants, who barged in, all wearing
outfits from Jack Frost's new designer
label, Ice Blue. Jack Frost had declared
that everyone should wear his range of
clothes, so they'd all look like him! Then,
with a crackling bolt of icy magic, he
had stolen the Fashion Fairies' seven
magical objects and vanished into the
human world.

Read Lola the Fashion Show Fairy to
find out what adventures are in store for Kirsty and Rachel!

Meet the Fashion Fairies

Miranda
the Beauty
Fairy

Claudia
the Accessories
Fairy

Tyra
the Dress Designer
Fairy

Alexa
the Fashion Reporter
Fairy

Matilda
the Hair Stylist
Fairy

Brooke
the Photographer
Fairy

Lola
the Fashion Show
Fairy

If Kirsty and Rachel don't find the Fashion Fairies'
magical objects, Jack Frost will ruin fashion forever!

www.rainbowmagicbooks.co.uk

RAINBOW magic

Meet the fairies, play games
and get sneak peeks at
the latest books!

www.rainbowmagicbooks.co.uk

There's fairy fun for everyone on
our wonderful website.
You'll find great activities, competitions, stories and
fairy profiles, and also a special newsletter.

Get 30% off all Rainbow Magic books at
www.rainbowmagicbooks.co.uk

Enter the code RAINBOW at the checkout.
Offer ends 31 December 2012.

Offer valid in United Kingdom and Republic of Ireland only.

Competition!

Here's a friend who Kirsty and Rachel met in an earlier story. Use the clues below to help you guess her name. When you have enjoyed all seven of the Fashion Fairies books, arrange the first letters of each mystery fairy's name to make a special word, then send us the answer!

CLUES

1. This fairy has the number 7 on her top.

2. She loves to play sports!

3. One of her items is a magical bicycle bell.

The fairy's name is _ _ _ _ _ _ _ the _ _ _ _ _ Fairy

We will put all of the correct entries into a draw and select one winner to receive a special Fashion Fairies goody bag. Your name will also be featured in a forthcoming Rainbow Magic story!

Enter online now at www.rainbowmagicbooks.co.uk

No purchase required. Only one entry per child. Two prize draws will take place on 31 May 2013 and 31 August 2013. Alternatively readers can send the answers on a postcard to: Rainbow Magic Fashion Fairies Competition, Orchard Books, 338 Euston Road, London, NW1 3BH. Australian readers can write to: Rainbow Magic Fashion Fairies Competition, Hachette Children's Books, Level 17/207 Kent St, Sydney, NSW 2000. E-mail: childrens.books@hachette.com.au.
New Zealand readers should write to Rainbow Magic Fashion Fairies Competition, 4 Whetu Place, Mairangi Bay, Auckland, NZ

The Complete Book of Fairies

Packed with secret fairy facts
and extra-special rainbow reveals, this magical guide
includes all you need to know about your favourite
Rainbow Magic friends.

Out Now!